CENA & ORTON:
RIVALRY IN THE RING

BY TRACEY WEST

Grosset & Dunlap
An Imprint of Penguin Group (USA) Inc.

GROSSET & DUNLAP
Published by the Penguin Group
Penguin Group (USA) Inc., 375 Hudson Street, New York, New York 10014, USA
Penguin Group (Canada), 90 Eglinton Avenue East, Suite 700,
Toronto, Ontario M4P 2Y3, Canada
(a division of Pearson Penguin Canada Inc.)
Penguin Books Ltd., 80 Strand, London WC2R 0RL, England
Penguin Group Ireland, 25 St. Stephen's Green, Dublin 2, Ireland
(a division of Penguin Books Ltd.)
Penguin Group (Australia), 250 Camberwell Road, Camberwell, Victoria 3124, Australia
(a division of Pearson Australia Group Pty. Ltd.)
Penguin Books India Pvt. Ltd., 11 Community Centre, Panchsheel Park,
New Delhi—110 017, India
Penguin Group (NZ), 67 Apollo Drive, Rosedale, North Shore 0632, New Zealand
(a division of Pearson New Zealand Ltd.)
Penguin Books (South Africa) (Pty.) Ltd., 24 Sturdee Avenue,
Rosebank, Johannesburg 2196, South Africa

Penguin Books Ltd., Registered Offices: 80 Strand, London WC2R 0RL, England

ISBN 978-0-448-45609-6   10 9 8 7 6 5 4 3 2

WWE Superstars John Cena and Randy Orton have both accomplished so much in sports entertainment. But ever since they joined the WWE, their destinies have been linked.

Both Superstars burst onto
the scene in 2002, just months apart.
Randy Orton showed up on *SmackDown*
in April and faced Hardcore Holly.
Fans were astounded to see the
newcomer leap off the top rope
and then pin Holly for the win!

Two months later, former WWE Champion Kurt Angle issued a challenge: Which WWE newcomer had the guts to face him in the ring? John Cena answered the call. He dominated Angle for most of the match, covering him again and again for attempted pins. In the end, Kurt Angle won, but the fans were impressed with the rookie's guts and skills.

Cena and Orton quickly rose to the top of the ranks in the WWE. Randy Orton formed a tag team with Edge called Rated-RKO. Cena became the WWE Champion. The two Superstars were friendly rivals—until 2007. That January, Mr. McMahon pitted Cena and Shawn Michaels in a match against Rated-RKO for the World Tag

It was a heated match. Cena pinned Orton for the win, giving Cena and Michaels the Tag Team Championship. Orton and Edge vowed revenge on Cena. The seeds of a legendary rivalry had been planted.

Cena was a double champion, and everyone wanted a piece of him—even his new tag team partner, Shawn Michaels. Michaels tried to steal the WWE Championship from Cena at WrestleMania 23, but lost.

Then Mr. McMahon made the tag team defend their championship during a 10-Man Battle Royal on *Raw*. Michaels shocked the crowd by tossing Cena—his own partner—over the top rope!

Now Cena was in a rivalry against Shawn Michaels, Randy Orton, and Edge. At Backlash 2007, the Superstars battled in a Fatal 4-Way Match. Orton tried to stop Cena with his signature move, the RKO, but Cena pushed him off. Orton collided with Edge and then fell to the floor. Michaels nailed Cena with a superkick. Cena landed on top of Randy Orton—and then pinned him for the win. It looked like nobody could take the championship from John Cena!

But Randy Orton was not going to back down. As a rookie, he had dubbed himself the Legend Killer. John Cena was becoming one of the biggest legends the WWE had ever seen. If anyone could topple Cena, it was Orton.

The next time the two Superstars faced off was in a non-title match on May 7, 2007. Orton was pumped for the match. "My career, my title hopes, and my life get back on track tonight," he said.

Orton brought his best to the ring that night, but The Great Khali interrupted the match. He attacked Cena and walked away with the stolen championship belt—but not the title.

With The Great Khali also gunning for Cena, Orton chose a new strategy. On *Raw* on July 23, 2007, Cena was celebrating a victory in the ring. *Bam!* Randy Orton snuck up behind him and delivered an RKO, slamming the stunned champ into the mat.

A week later, Orton tried a different tactic. He sat in a folding chair outside the ring while Cena battled Carlito on *Raw*. Orton distracted Cena so much that it cost him the match! Orton's message was clear: He wouldn't stop his assault on Cena until he had a chance to take the title from him.

Randy Orton finally got his wish at SummerSlam 2007. Just days before the event, he attacked Cena with two more vicious RKOs. Cena did not enter the ring in top form. Right from the start, Orton focused his attacks on Cena's weakened neck. To the millions of fans watching, it looked like Orton would finally walk away with the WWE Championship he wanted so badly.

Orton pinned Cena to the mat. The ref counted, "One . . . two . . ." But Cena lifted his shoulder off of the mat before the ref could finish counting! The stunned crowd watched as Cena rose to his feet and hoisted Orton onto his back. Then he pounded Orton into the mat with an Attitude Adjustment.

The Legend Killer had done his best, but he *still* couldn't take down the champ!

Randy Orton demanded another rematch, but Mr. McMahon wouldn't give it to him. Angry, Orton attacked John Cena's father on *Raw*! Now it was Cena who wanted to face Orton again—for revenge. The match was set for Unforgiven on September 16, 2007.

Orton had high hopes of defeating Cena in this match. But when the bell rang, Cena attacked Orton with a fury the fans had never seen. The ref ordered him to stop his assault on Orton, but Cena refused. The match ended in a disqualification. Once again, Orton left the ring without the championship.

Two weeks later, Cena faced Mr. Kennedy in a match on *Raw*. Cena won, but Orton flattened him with a surprise attack outside the ring. Cena walked away with a serious injury: a torn tendon. Doctors said it could

At No Mercy on October 7, Mr. McMahon stripped Cena of the WWE Championship. He was injured and out of the WWE for the foreseeable future. The longest championship reign in nineteen years had come to an end. Mr. McMahon handed the championship over to Orton. He defended it twice against Triple H that night and ultimately walked away victorious.

At the beginning of 2008, Randy Orton was on top of the world. He still held the championship. John Cena was just a bad memory.

But at the Royal Rumble on January 27, something happened that shocked Randy Orton—and the entire WWE. Only Triple H and Batista were left in the ring. It was time for the thirtieth man to enter. Who was it? John Cena, back from his injury!

"Come and get some," the Champ challenged. He took out both Superstars and won the Rumble. Four months after his injury, Cena was back. And he wanted only one thing: to destroy Randy Orton and win back the championship.

Winning the Royal Rumble meant that John Cena could face Randy Orton at the next WrestleMania. But Cena couldn't wait. He showed up on *Raw* the next night and challenged Orton to an on-the-spot title match.

"Who wants WrestleMania to come early?" Cena asked the fans. But Orton refused. Mr. McMahon stepped in and booked the match for No Way Out.

During the match, Orton hurt his knee. He slid out of the ring, hoping to lose by disqualification—and keep the championship. Cena went after the injured Superstar, but Orton recovered and pounded him with an RKO. Orton slid back into the ring, sure he'd won. But Cena recovered and came after him once again. Panicked, Orton started attacking the ref. The match ended, and Orton got the disqualification he wanted.

When WrestleMania XXIV rolled around, Cena was anxious to fight. But there was another Superstar gunning for the championship: Triple H.

Orton was determined to see his "one-man dynasty" continue. He used strategy, letting Cena and Triple H do the work for him. After Triple H downed Cena with a Pedigree, Orton saw his chance and kicked Triple H in the head. Then he pinned Triple H, winning the match—and keeping the gold!

John Cena spent the next year trying to get his championship back. The rivalry led up to Breaking Point on September 13, 2009. Mr. McMahon pitted the Superstars against each other in an "I Quit" Match. There would be no disqualifications, no pinfalls, no count outs. The only way to win would be for one Superstar to get the other to say "I quit!"

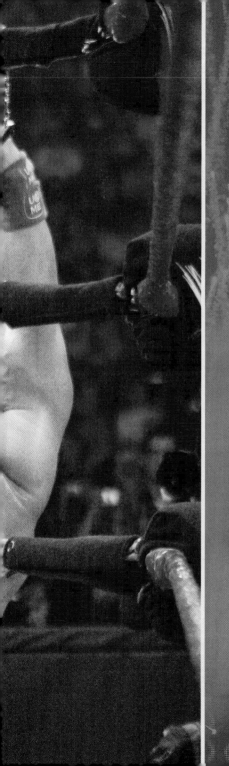

As the fierce match raged on, Orton and Cena punished each other with one devastating attack after another. In the end, Cena handcuffed Orton to him, twisting his opponent's body into a painful position. He hated to do it, but Orton had no choice. He spat out the dreaded words: "I quit." Once again, Cena held the WWE Championship.

But Randy Orton was not about to walk away and leave the championship behind. He faced his biggest rival again just weeks later on October 4, 2009. For this match, the foes were locked in a steel cage with no escape.

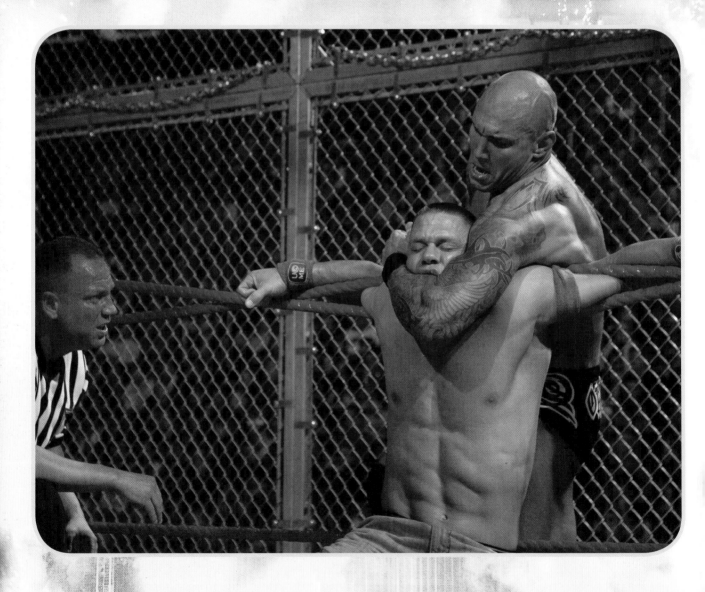

Orton's hunger for victory fueled him that night. He delivered a devastating RKO, sending Cena crashing to the mat. When Cena fell to the mat unconscious, Orton made the pin for the win. Once again, the championship changed hands.

Fans were beginning to wonder: Would this rivalry ever end? And which Superstar would end up on top?

Mr. McMahon decided it was time to answer the question once and for all. He scheduled a sixty-minute Iron Man Match at Bragging Rights. In an Iron Man Match, anything goes. The winner is the Superstar who gets the most pinfalls before the hour is up.

The bell rang and one of the most brutal hours in WWE history began. Orton used every trick he had. He assaulted Cena with a TV monitor. His friends entered the bout to help him. He even tried to attack Cena with fireworks!

But Cena stayed strong, fighting off every onslaught. In the end, Orton pinned Cena five times . . . and Cena pinned Orton six times. The Champ was back—for good.

It looked like the legendary rivalry was finally over. But as fans of the WWE know, friends can become foes in an instant. Whatever happens, John Cena and Randy Orton's epic battles for the gold will never be forgotten.